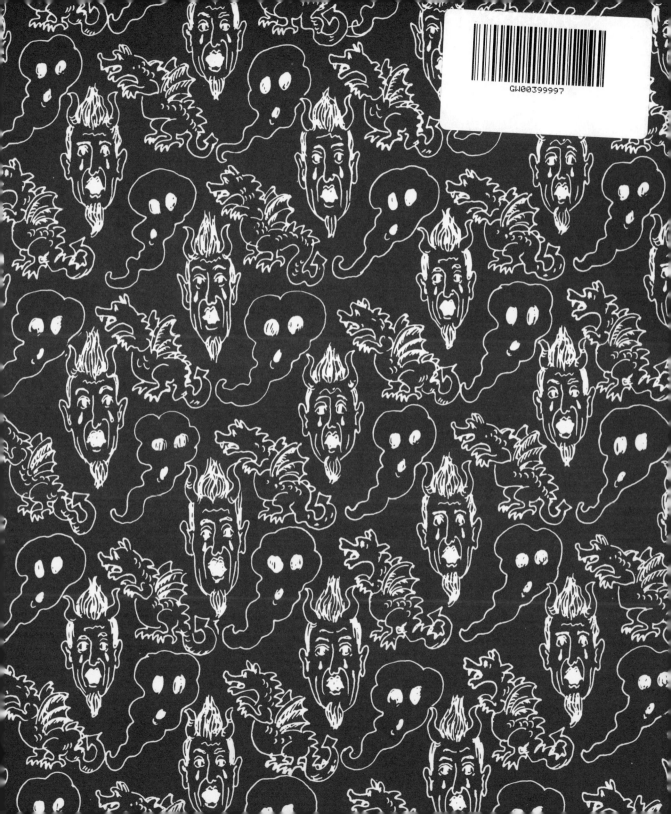

GW00399997

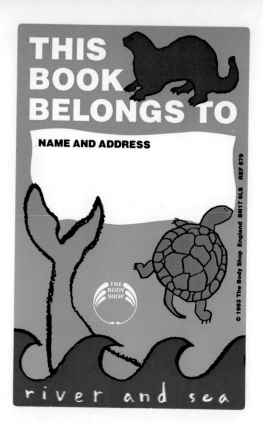

THIS
BOOK
BELONGS TO

NAME AND ADDRESS

river and sea

One Night At Lottie's House

Max Dann

Illustrated by David Pearson

Melbourne
Oxford University Press
Oxford Auckland New York

Arthur looked under the bed. No sign of any burglars or man-eating spiders there. Then he checked inside the wardrobe for vampires and warlocks. No, nothing there either.

Arthur upturned a pair of armchairs, looking for werewolves. He searched through drawers for goblins. He checked the mantlepiece for poisonous snakes, then he stared up inside the fireplace for concealed zombies, and examined the walls for hidden doors.

He felt around for wet footprints on the carpet to find out
if a 2000-year-old amphibian had recently crossed the floor.
He peered behind the old picture-frames and he climbed up
on to a chair to feel around the highest bookshelves. Arthur
checked every corner of the room. Ghosts and trolls can hide
anywhere.

Arthur consulted his book *Demons, Monsters and Ghosts* to make sure he had covered it all, then placed a ring of fresh garlic cloves around his bed. He slipped a silver whistle around his neck, and put on his running shoes to wear to bed. His suitcase, beside him on the floor, was filled with everything he might need: special herbs, wooden stakes, heavy rope, handcuffs, magnifying-glass, one vampire mirror, first-aid kit, ping-pong bat, invisible ink (for leaving messages when kidnapped), and his ghost-fighting kit.

These were normal precautions for Arthur when he had to spend a night away from home. He did not like sleeping anywhere else but in his own bedroom. Other people's spare bedrooms were full of unknown dangers. He had stayed with aunts whose small, musty houses were full of faceless shadows. He had stayed overnight with uncles whose dim, dusty rooms smelt of strange things. But he had never stayed anywhere as big, and eerie, and run-down as Lottie's house.

Lottie was Arthur's friend from school. She seemed
a normal and decent girl – but Arthur didn't care. He had
thrown himself at his parents' feet and pleaded with them to
take him along to his father's annual dentists' convention.
He'd promised to behave perfectly and stay in the hotel room
the whole time, reading quietly.

Arthur's father had said: 'You're too short to be a dentist, son. You can stay over at Lottie's house instead. We'll pick you up first thing in the morning.'

'Please, please!' Arthur had said.

'It's only for one night, Arthur. I'm sure you'll have lots of fun.'

Arthur's father had dropped him off at Lottie's gate. Arthur had only needed one look at the house before saying: 'I don't think I'll be having any fun, Father. I don't think I'll live through to the morning!'

But Arthur's father had just helped him with his suitcase as far as the front gate, hugged him goodbye, and driven away.

The house was so big that it took up three blocks. It was so high it blocked out half the sky. Windows were cracked, and shutters hung loose. It was built from wood that had turned to splinters. The paint had dried up and blown away, and had left it a shade of dull grey.

Arthur walked very carefully through the front yard. If he stepped into a crevice, he thought, he would probably never be found again. There were big cracks splitting open the ground where grass should have been. There were thistles and weeds growing, and a lot of trees. Some of the trees were nothing more than skeletons without leaves, others climbed and stood like gigantic, twisted monsters, leaves swishing and calling out in the wind.

When Arthur reached the front porch he saw there were scratch marks on the door. They looked like the claw marks of wild animals. Arthur knocked quietly. If nobody heard him, he thought, he would just have to go back home.

But Lottie was expecting him. She heaved open the creaking door and said: 'Arthur! Welcome! Come on in and make yourself at home.'

Lottie's house was nothing like Arthur's house. The hallway was dark, and the air felt cold. The carpet was worn and the walls were streaked in stains of faded yellow. The furniture looked old and broken, and the light switches were sticky to touch.

The house had more spare rooms than any other kind of room: mysterious, abandoned rooms that opened into black, winding corridors. There were rooms leading into other rooms that led to even further rooms. The stairs were dirty and old, and they all squeaked — except for the fifth step, which wasn't there at all.

Lottie told him to leave his suitcase at the top of the stairs. 'Your room isn't tidied up yet. Come down and meet my parents, they're a lot of fun. It's dinner time, anyway.'

When Arthur met Lottie's mother and father he was struck speechless. They were fiends or perhaps aliens who had been sent from another planet to take over the earth. Lottie's mother tap-danced around the kitchen while she cooked dinner, and did a pirouette at the refrigerator. Lotties's father sat at the table stomping his foot and playing a harmonica, offkey. He had long hair down the sides of his head but none at all on top, and owned a 2.5 metre rubber tree he called Orson. Lottie's father's teeth looked like they hadn't been cleaned for a few days. (Arthur cleaned *his* teeth six times a day, even if he happened to be not eating.)

Dinner looked like fried frogs' bodies and lizards' legs in lettuce leaves.

'Aren't you hungry?' Lottie's mother asked. Arthur was staring silently at his plate.

'Once you start eating, you'll love it,' Lottie's father said.

'Pumpkin patties with bean sprout salad. Yum!' Lottie exclaimed.

Arthur still couldn't eat.

'How about I make you a sandwich?' Lottie's father asked. He cut two slices of bread as thick as concrete slabs and made Arthur a big toasted sandwich with peanut butter and some cold spaghetti thrown in. Arthur ate his sandwich and tried not to look while the others ate their food.

At home, Arthur always watched TV after dinner. He usually watched *Love Cruise* on Friday nights. But Lottie's father wanted to watch a horror film about plants that grew legs and walked about eating people who were in their way. Lottie's father thought it was a comedy and laughed a lot. Lottie's mother sat a table in the corner and made hats out of coloured paper.

'Okay, kids, time for bed.' Lottie's father clapped his hands. 'You'd better get to bed before the bunyip gets you!'

Arthur knew a bit about bunyips. The bunyip lived in swamps or lagoons, but Arthur hadn't realized there were swamps in Lottie's neighbourhood. He had seen a large muddy patch in the front garden on the way in, though.

When Lottie showed Arthur his room he thought he was going to faint. Arthur had expected the room to be untidy; few people managed to keep a room as neat as he did. But not even in his most frightening nightmares had he seen a room like this one. His suitcase was the only neat and tidy object there. The floorboards shifted and groaned when he stepped on them, and the windows were so grimy you almost couldn't see outside. There was dusty junk piled up to the ceiling in cluttered, shadowy stacks. There were cracks crawling up and down the walls, and draughts blowing in, fluttering the cobwebs overhead.

Lottie's room next door looked even worse. It was full of test tubes and beakers and bunsen burners for her scientific experiments. Lottie told Arthur to knock three times on the wall if he wanted anything. What Arthur wanted was to go home.

Back in his own room, Arthur made certain he had checked everywhere before deciding it was safe to go to sleep. He put on his elephant pyjamas, set the alarm clock for six, and climbed into bed. Arthur's father had said he would pick him up at seven and Arthur wanted to be sure he would be ready.

Arthur closed his eyes tight and did his best to pretend he was not really in Lottie's house. If he thought hard enough he could imagine he was back safe in his cosy, tidy bedroom instead. He could almost see his sports-car wallpaper around him, and hear the soft purring of tiny car motors. And, if he concentrated even harder, he could nearly smell the jasmine that grew outside his bedroom window.

Thinking he was back in his own room made him sleepy. His eyelids grew heavier and heavier, then —

CREEEEK! KAWREEAK!

Arthur sat up as straight as the bedpost. There was something creeping about up on the roof!

CROOORREEEAK!

There it was again! Right over his head! Was it a giant rat as big as a hippopotamus? Or perhaps one of the stone gargoyles had come to life? Arthur thought of the worst. He carefully turned around and tapped three times on Lottie's wall.

'Lottie?' he whispered loudly. 'Lottie, are you awake? There's something walking on the roof!'

'I can't hear anything, Arthur. Go back to sleep,' Lottie called back.

CREEEAK!

'There! Did you hear it then?' Arthur said.

'That's just the house, silly. It creaks and moves around like that all the time. Timber houses creak.'

Arthur's house didn't move around. It was made of brick.

Arthur lay awake for a long time, looking out for dark shapes creeping around his bed. He couldn't actually see anything moving, but then, out of the darkness came a crackling, rustling noise followed by a sharp snapping noise. Then silence. The noises had come from Lottie's room. Arthur leant over and pressed his ear to the wall. He heard the noises again! The same crackling and rustling and sharp snapping, as if — burning wood! Yes, that's what it sounded like! Fire! The house was on fire!

Arthur ran straight out of his room and into Lottie's. She was sitting up in bed reading *The Hound of the Baskervilles* and sucking boiled humbugs. She was unwrapping the cellophane from another one when he rushed in. The noise had just been the cellophane wrappers crackling!

'Sorry, Arthur, I would have offered you one, but I thought you would've been asleep by now,' Lottie said.

Sleep! Sleep? How could anyone sleep in this house? Arthur asked himself once he was back in bed. He tried closing his eyes and thinking of sheep, but all he could see were flying lizards.

Then, out of the darkness —

SHE BA BI DO WAH! SHABOOM BA SHABOOM!

Arthur leapt up into the air, and landed under the bed. Now they were being attacked! Somebody had gone crazy downstairs!

BOOM BA BE BA DO SHOOWEE!

Arthur had never heard or felt anything like it before. The floor was vibrating, the bed was shaking — the house was in the grip of some unseen force!

WAH WAH SHABOOM WAH WO WAHAHAHEHEE!

Yelling and shouting! Pounding jungle drums! The house was possessed by wild native spirits. Arthur rapped on Lottie's wall again.

'Lottie! We're being attacked! Get out while you can!'

'Relax, Arthur, it's just my mother and father,' Lottie said. 'They get a kick out of playing their old rock-and-roll records up loud. They'll go to bed soon.'

Arthur's mother and father listened to Frank Sinatra, with the volume turned down low.

Arthur sat up reading *Demons, Monsters and Ghosts*. And long after the record player had been switched off and Lottie's mother and father had gone to bed, Arthur was still awake reading. He was up to the story about a giant cat that had terrorized an entire town in 1466, and disappeared without leaving a trace. It looked a lot like Lottie's cat, except that it was a different colour. Lottie called her cat Stewart. The cat in the story didn't have a name. Arthur went on reading. A garage door slammed shut in the wind, and a dog howled at the moon. Arthur tried not to listen.

TAP! TAP! TAP!

There was something tapping at the window. Arthur went on reading.

SCREEEECH!

Now it was scratching! Arthur closed his book and crawled underneath the bed covers.

SCRAWWCH! TAP! TAP!

Arthur pretended not to hear.

TAP! SCREEACH! TAP! TAP!

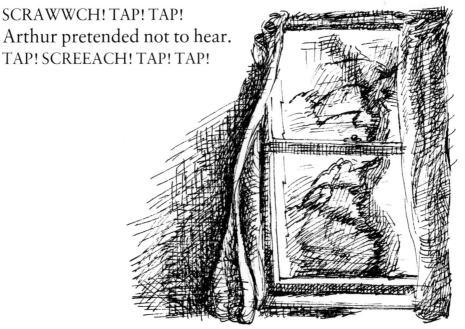

Arthur had to get up and see. He slid out of the sheets and on to the floor. He crept across to the wall on all fours, so that he couldn't be seen. The last few steps, he crawled. He came to the window and drew the curtain aside, just enough to get a peep. Oh, it was terrible! Horrible! It was the ugliest sight he had ever seen!

There was a hand tapping and scraping the glass. It was not even a whole hand, just a single finger, long, twisted and gnarled, begging to get inside. It came from out of the darkness, and reached back, way back, where it joined on to — a tree? A branch of a tree. That was all it was, just a — *Thud!* Now there was a noise coming from the hall! Something rattled and clanged. Then there was the sound of footsteps scuffing past Arthur's door. Slow, heavy feet. Arthur tiptoed across, put his eye to the keyhole, and looked out into the corridor.

Arthur reeled and had to lean back against the wall to steady himself after what he saw. He'd only caught a glimpse of it before it disappeared past his door, but Arthur was sure he'd seen a pair of legs, men's pyjamas legs, slowly walking the length of the hall. Arthur knew too who belonged to the body that was attached to those legs. It was Lottie's father! And, in his hand dangled a heavy chain that dragged along behind him on the floor.

It took Arthur only a moment for his trained mind to reach a conclusion about what he had seen. He had been wrong all along. Lottie's father wasn't an alien or a fiend. He was a ghost!

Arthur had read that ghosts walked along halls at night and often carried chains as well. No wonder Lottie's father looked so pale and thin! Arthur shuddered at what he'd discovered. Lottie's father was actually dead, a ghost, an apparition, forced to wander along corridors, night after night. A haunted, tortured soul, dragging a chain behind him that had probably held him prisoner, in a secret dungeon long ago.

Arthur should have realized earlier that Lottie's father was a ghost. He'd read that ghosts have poor teeth, and Arthur, son of a dentist, should have seen this right away. Lottie's father: an average human being by day, a lost and lonely ghost by night.

Arthur panicked. He ran across to the bed and rapped
on the wall. There was nothing but silence from Lottie's side
of the wall. He unpacked his ghost-kit, and peeked out into
the corridor. When he was sure there was no sign of Lottie's
father, he dashed out and went to open Lottie's door. It
would not open. He knocked, but Lottie did not answer. She
had locked it from the inside, and had stuck a wad of
cottonwool in each ear. How else was she going to get to sleep
with Arthur next door?

Arthur knocked again, but when there was no answer
again, he crept away down the hall. If he couldn't save Lottie,
he would have to be content with saving himself.

Arthur reached the top of the stairs, and strained to see
down into the night's gloom. He had to reach the kitchen if he
was going to make the special drink that would make him
safe from ghosts. It seemed quiet downstairs and he could not
hear a rattling chain now anywhere.

Arthur unpacked his ghost-fighting kit and took out a bag full of toe-nail clippings. They came with instructions:

Spread three toe-nail clippings for every step in dread. Done this way, no meeting with the dead.

Arthur put down exactly three toe-nail clippings for every step he took: down the stairs, along a passage, through the lounge-room, and across the hallway. Once he thought he heard a clanging, so he took a sprig of mistletoe out of his kit and held it in his left hand, as the instruction book said. But the noise was soft and sounded as if it came from the back shed outside.

Arthur reached the kitchen and laid his ghost-fighting kit on the kitchen table. There was no time to waste. Arthur had to quickly make and drink the potion, as directed. It was an ancient recipe full of ancient things, passed down through generations. One drink, and the ghost would find Arthur completely repulsive.

Arthur found a large bowl, spread the instruction book open in front of him and read:

Keep a clear head. Place twelve dried snails' shells in a bowl while standing with your back to the west.

Arthur looked on the shelves, but all he could find were almonds. He used them instead.

Do not listen to one word
the ghost says.
Add one small spoonful of
wild beast.

Arthur couldn't find any of that either. He used a teaspoon of yeast.

Keep one eye closed, one hand
on the chest, sprinkle ground
bat's dust and the shrivelled
whiskers of ten old men.

The nearest Arthur could get was a half a cup of coconut and a dash of nutmeg.

A handful of sawdust from a
coffin and weeds that grow by
a graveyard fence.

Bran looked like sawdust and parsley would do for weeds that grow near a graveyard fence. He used goat's milk instead of wolf's milk, honey for swamp goo, vanilla essence for holy water, and two prunes — he wasn't going to eat cockroaches.

Next he had to stir it for a day while chanting in Latin. Arthur shut the door and switched on the blender. After all his work, he was starting to feel tired. The drink was ready in a minute and Arthur poured himself a little. It tasted quite good, like a milkshake. He took another sip and yawned. Even though it wasn't the exact recipe, he felt sure it would work.

The house was very quiet. Arthur took one more sip; he was feeling quite sleepy. The glass he had filled was empty but he couldn't remember drinking it, probably because he was so tired. He sat watching the glass. First it swam, then it faded, and then it disappeared altogether . . . Arthur had fallen asleep.

'*Um, ummmm*. This drink is delicious.'

These were the first words Arthur heard when he woke up. He had fallen asleep in the kitchen, the sun was up, and Lottie's father was standing over him, drinking a glassful of the potion. 'I hope you don't mind, Arthur, I tried some of your drink.'

Lottie and her mother were sitting at the table as well, in their dressing-gowns. They too had a glassful each.

'Isn't it great?' Lottie said.

'Heavenly,' Lottie's mother agreed.

Lottie's father went to get a refill. 'I hope you don't mind, Arthur, if I just have a little more.'

'No, no!' Arthur said. 'If you drink it, it will have no effect. It's not meant for ghosts themselves.'

Lottie and her family sat in stunned silence. They had not realized Arthur was so rude. He had no manners at all.

'I know you're a ghost!' Arthur stood up and said to Lottie's father. 'I saw you last night. You walked past my door dragging a chain along on the floor.'

'I'm sorry, did I wake you? I was on my way down to the back shed,' Lottie's father said.

'You *know* you're a ghost?' Arthur was shocked.

'I was going down to lock up my pushbike.'

'He forgets to do it every second night,' Lottie said. 'The last one was stolen.'

Arthur was too embarrassed to have any breakfast. He felt too foolish to eat. Besides, it took him half an hour to vacuum up the toe-nail clippings he had dropped all over the floor.

When Arthur's father came to pick him up, Arthur was standing by the front door with his suitcase. He was too embarrassed to speak. He ran down the front path and locked himself in the car. He would never be able to look Lottie and her parents in the eye again.

But Lottie and her mother and father didn't mind. The drink he had made was just delicious. Lottie's father had made Arthur copy out the recipe for them before he left.

They stood on the front porch and waved goodbye to Arthur. Lottie's mother did it standing on her head. Arthur could see them all out the back window of the car.

'By golly, that Arthur's a strange boy,' Lottie's father said. He was looking at the recipe.

'He seemed very normal and decent at school,' Lottie said.

'Where do you suppose I can buy the shrivelled whiskers of ten old men?'

OXFORD UNIVERSITY PRESS

Oxford Toronto
Delhi Bombay Calcutta Madras Karachi
Kuala Lumpur Singapore Hong Kong Tokyo
Nairobi Dar es Salaam Cape Town
Melbourne Auckland
and associates in
Beirut Berlin Ibadan Nicosia

National Library of Australia
Cataloguing-in-Publication data:

Dann, Max, 1955-
  One night at Lottie's house.

  For children.
  ISBN 0 19 554637 7.

  1. Children's stories
  I. Pearson, David. II. Title.

A823'.3

Typeset in 14 point Sabon by Bookset, Melbourne
Printed in Hong Kong
Published by Oxford University Press, 7 Bowen Crescent, Melbourne
OXFORD is a trademark of Oxford University Press